The Pigeon Wants a Puppy!

for **Nelson**
(good boy)

ISBN-13: 978-0-545-15514-4
ISBN-10: 0-545-15514-2

12 11 10 9 8 7 6 5 4 3 2 1   9 10 11 12 13 14/0

Printed in the U.S.A.   40

First Scholastic printing, January 2009

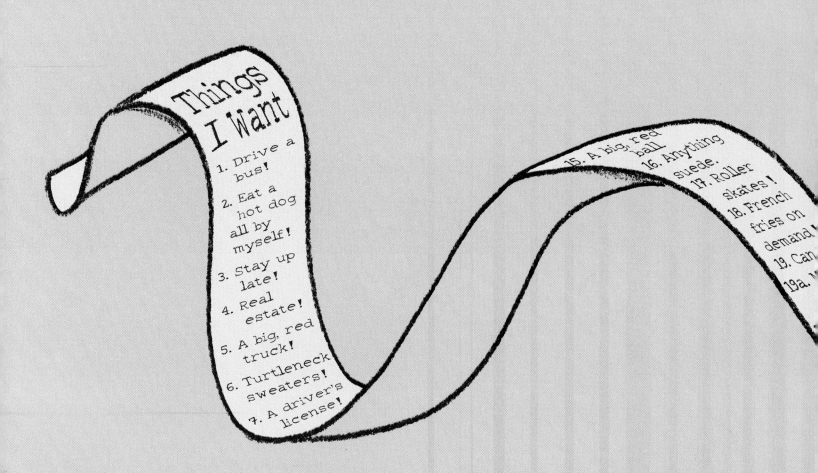

Things I Want

1. Drive a bus!
2. Eat a hot dog all by myself!
3. Stay up late!
4. Real estate!
5. A big, red truck!
6. Turtleneck sweaters!
7. A driver's license!

15. A big, red ball
16. Anything suede.
17. Roller skates!
18. French fries on demand!
19. Can
19a. M

The Pigeon Wants a Puppy!

words and pictures by mo willems

SCHOLASTIC INC.
New York Toronto London Auckland Sydney
Mexico City New Delhi Hong Kong Buenos Aires

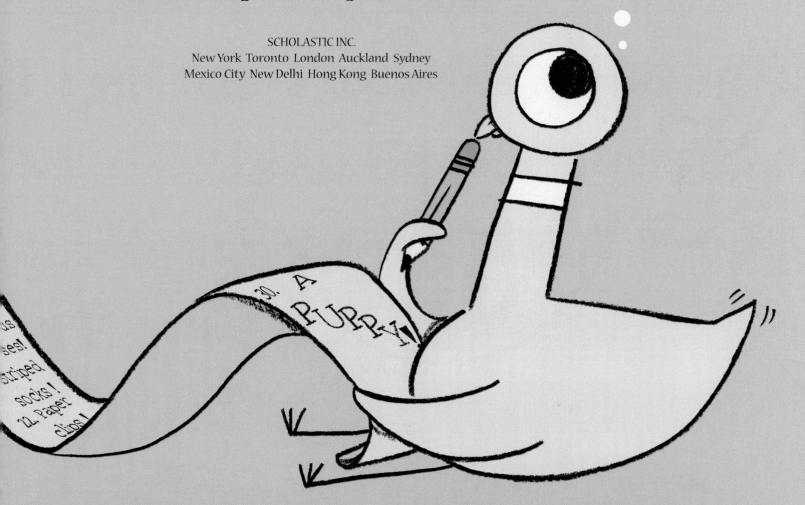

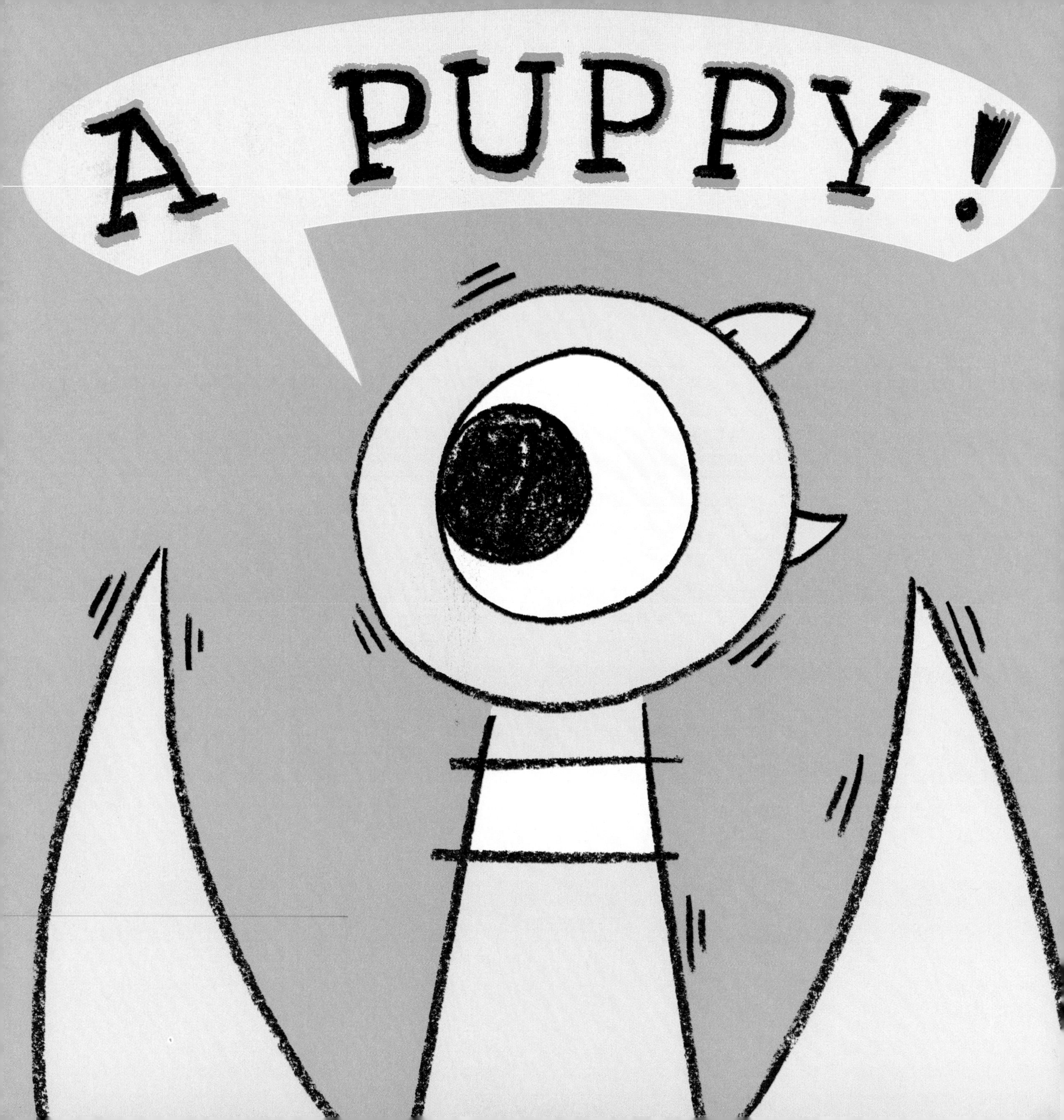
A PUPPY!

I WANT
A PUPPY!
RIGHT HERE!
RIGHT NOW!

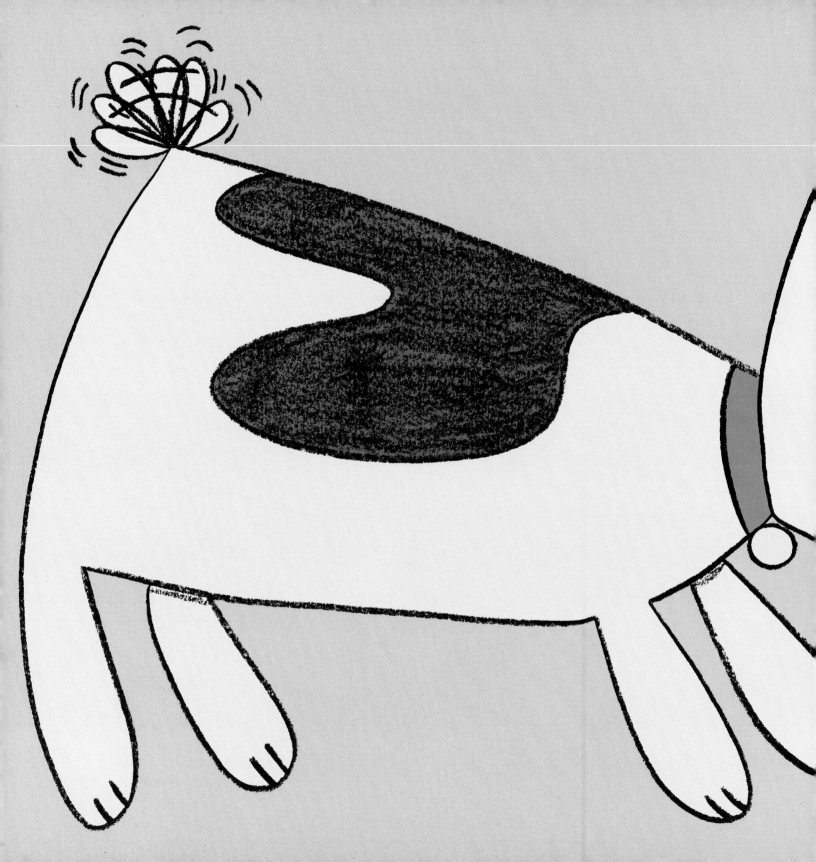

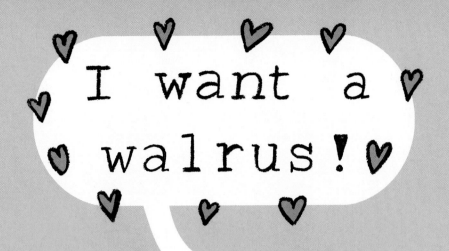